S0-BSP-723

WITHDRAWN

J.R. JAMERSON MEM. LIB.
157 Main Street
P.O. Box 789
Appomattox, Va 24522
(434) 352-5340

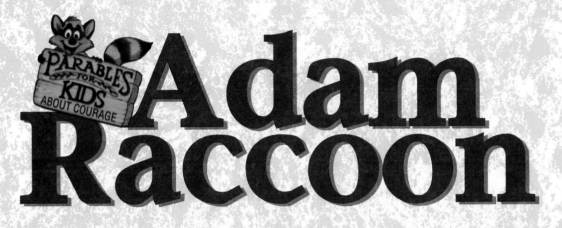

Adam Raccoon

and
Bully Garumph

Glen Keane

Chariot Books™
*A Division of Cook
Communications Ministries*

To Julia and Spencer

Chariot Books™ is an imprint of Chariot Family Publishing
Cook Communications Ministries, Elgin, Illinois 60120
Cook Communications Ministries, Paris, Ontario
Kingsway Communications, Eastbourne, England

ADAM RACCOON AND BULLY GARUMPH
© 1995 by Glen Keane for text and illustrations

All rights reserved. Except for brief excerpts for review purposes,
no part of this book may be reproduced or used in any form without written
permission from the publisher.
First printing, 1995
Printed in the United States of America
99 98 97 96 95   5 4 3 2 1

Painted by Yakovetic

Library of Congress Cataloging-in-Publication Data

Keane, Glen
Adam Raccoon and bully Garumph / Glen Keane.
p. cm. — (Parables for kids)
Summary: Adam Raccoon learns to love his enemy, the bully Garumph Bear,
 rather than fighting him.
ISBN 1-55513-367-3
[1. Bullies—Fiction. 2. Conduct of life—Fiction.] I. Title. II. Series: Keane, Glen,
Parables for kids.
PZ7.K2173Ab 1995
[E]—dc20
                                                                    95-21894
                                                                       CIP
                                                                        AC

Scriptures quoted from the *International Children's Bible,* New Century Version,
copyright © 1983, 1986, 1988 by Word Publishing, Dallas, Texas 75039.
Used by permission.

As springtime came,
the Master's Wood Soccer
Tournament was underway.
The game was into its final
moments. Shouts and
cheers filled the air.

With the score tied,
Adam Raccoon raced down
the field with the ball.

He had a clear shot
and prepared for
the kick.

The crowd watched
anxiously, when
suddenly . . .

a big foot stuck out,
tripping Adam.

The crowd gasped.

"Oh, my.
What have I done?!"
Garumph the Bear said.
"I've got such big feet.

Here.
Let me help you up."

And with a yank,
Adam flew through
the air . . .

and into the net.

The referee raced
in blowing his whistle.

"You're not calling a foul
on me, are you?"
Garumph bellowed.

"Well, no, no . . . I . . . I
guess I made a mistake,"
the ref replied.

"Well! Don't let it
happen again. I hate it
when people don't play fair."

And before anybody could stop him, Garumph kicked the winning goal.

Adam was furious
as the other team
cheered and carried
Garumph off on their
shoulders.

Later that night as King Aren, the mighty lion, was tucking him into bed, Adam said, "Garumph is such a bully!

"Adam, if you really
want to be like me,
instead of hating him,
try loving him."

"Loving him!" Adam
cried. "But that's
impossible. I can't
love Garumph!"

Over milk and cookies, King Aren explained. "Adam, anyone can love his friends. But it takes a special kind of courageous love to love your enemies."

Adam lay in bed
that night wondering
if he had the special
kind of love that
King Aren had.

The next day dawned
bright and cheerful.
"Hope your team
wins today!"
Adam's friends
greeted him.

"Thanks!"
Adam called out.

"On such a nice day maybe it won't be so hard to love even Garumph," he said to himself. He didn't notice Garumph's foot in his path.

Down the bank and into the stream he tumbled.

SPLASH

"HA HA HA! Boy, are you clumsy," laughed Garumph. "No wonder you lost the game."

In a flash, Adam
started punching
and kicking Garumph
with all his might.

Bellowing with rage,
Garumph chased Adam
across the bridge.
"Wait'll I get my
hands on you!"

All through Master's
Wood they ran,

upsetting everyone
and everything
in their path.

"STOP!"
roared King Aren.

"Enough fighting!
Go home, both of you."

On the way back,
King Aren caught up
with Adam.
"I was going to love him,"
Adam explained.
"But before I could
even try I was so
upset I couldn't
stop myself."

"Adam, it's not easy.
It takes much more
courage to love
than to fight and hate.
Don't give up."

That afternoon
everyone showed up
to watch the final
soccer game.

Garumph was being
his usual unpleasant self.
But Adam kept his cool.

Adam congratulated him.
"Nice shot, Garumph!"

When Garumph's team ran out of water, Adam shared his water with them.

The game continued on. . . .
With the score tied
and only seconds to go,
Adam intercepted the ball.

Garumph, stunned by Adam's show of kindness, stood frozen while Adam raced toward the goal.

As time ran out,
with a mighty kick
Adam scored
the winning goal.

King Aren beamed
with pride as he watched
Adam and Garumph
shake hands.

"Now let me show you how to REALLY play soccer!" King Aren shouted.

"Come on, Garumph!" Adam said as they chased King Aren up and down the field, laughing.

REMEMBER THE STORY

Jesus said
"Love your enemies. Pray for those who hurt you. If you do this, then you will be true sons of your Father in heaven. Your Father causes the sun to rise on good people and bad people. . . ."
Matthew 5:44, 45

- How did Adam feel when Bully Garumph was mean to him? Have you ever felt like that? When? What happened?

- How did Adam act toward Bully Garumph at the beginning of the story? How did Adam act toward Bully Garumph at the end of the story?

- What did King Aren teach Adam about how to treat his enemy?

- Which took more courage and strength for Adam—to control his anger and be kind to Bully Garumph or to fight him? What did Adam learn about love?

- Why did King Aren want Adam to love Bully Garumph instead of fighting him?

- It's easy to love your friends and hard to love your enemies. Who is it hard for you to love? What can you do to show this person kindness? (A good place to start is to pray for this person.) Just as King Aren helped Adam, Jesus will give you the courage to love your enemies.